# Story Time for Little Porcupine

by Joseph Slate · illustrated by Jacqueline Rogers

Marshall Cavendish · New York

Text copyright © 2000 by Joseph Slate
Illustrations copyright © 2000 by Jacqueline Rogers
All rights reserved
Marshall Cavendish, 99 White Plains Road, Tarrytown, NY 10591
ISBN 0-7614-5073-4
Library of Congress Cataloging-in-Publication Data
Slate, Joseph
Story time for little porcupine / Joseph Slate ; illustrated by Jacqueline Rogers.
p.   cm.
Summary: Before he is ready to go to sleep, Little Porcupine wants to hear—and tell—stories
about the Big Porcupine in the Sky, the sun.
[1. Porcupines—Fiction. 2. Bedtime—Fiction. 3. Storytelling—Fiction.] I. Rogers, Jacqueline, ill. II. Title.
PZ7.S6289 Su 2001    [Fic]   99-055536

The text of this book is set in 16 point Esprit Book.
The illustrations are rendered in watercolor.
Printed in Hong Kong
1   3   5   6   4   2

For Martin John Garhart
—J.S.

For Emma
—J.R.

"It's sleepy time, Little Porcupine," says Mama Porcupine. She gives him a big ouchy hug.

"But first," says Little Porcupine, "it's story time. And it's Papa's turn to tell me a story."

"It is, it is," says Papa Porcupine. "It is indeed! But first, up to bed we go."

Little Porcupine climbs up on Papa Porcupine's back.

"Now, Papa," says Little Porcupine, "I want to hear a story about the Big Porcupine in the Sky. He's my favorite character in the whole wide world. I want to hear how the Big Porcupine got his spines."

"You do?" Papa Porcupine swings Little Porcupine onto his bed. "Well, grab your toes, 'cause here goes!"

## How the Big Porcupine Got His Spines

Once upon a time, the Big Porcupine in the Sky had no spines.
He was as bald as a pumpkin at high noon.

Bald or not, he was still the brightest star in the sky. He was the
Sun, the big bright Sun, the King of the Daytime Sky.

One day, a big thundercloud said to the other clouds: "Why does the Big Porcupine think he is King of the Sky? There is only one of him and many of us.

"If we put our heads together, we could cover him up for good. And then we could be the Kings of the Sky."

So the clouds rolled in from all over the sky.

They bumped and thumped and grump, grump, grumped. They clouded over Big Porcupine so well, not a single beam of light lit the earth.

But when clouds come together, there is more than just thumping and bumping, and grump, grump, grumping.

There is lightning. Big dagger bolts of lightning zigzag across the sky.

"Oh no, oh me, oh my," said Big Porcupine. "Lightning can't hurt me. But what if those big lightning bolts strike all the little porcupines on earth? It will hurt them. I must do something."

So he reached out with his great forepaws and caught every bolt that flashed from the clouds.

Soon, both his paws were full. What could he do?

Well, son, he flipped those lightning bolts up over his head, and began sticking them onto his bald head, his bald back, and his bald tail.

And that is how the Big Porcupine in the Sky got his spines.

Of course, we don't call them spines anymore. We call them the Sun's rays—beautiful rays that help make the rainbows span the sky.

"That was a good story," says Little Porcupine. "From now on, I will call my spines rays. And when my friends, the Little Creatures, ask me why, I will show-and-tell about the Big Porcupine in the Sky. But now, I am ready for another story."

"Another story," says Papa Porcupine. He scratches his head.

"Yes," says Little Porcupine. "And this one should be about a picnic that everyone gets invited to."

"Why is that?" asks Papa Porcupine.

"Because when Fox had a picnic, he did not invite me."

"Maybe he didn't have room," says Papa Porcupine.

"Maybe," says Little Porcupine. "But I bet if it was Big Porcupine's picnic he would make room for everybody."

"He would?"

"Yes," says Little Porcupine, "and I will tell you a story why. Do you want to hear it?"

"I am all spine-tingling ears," says Papa Porcupine.

"Okay," says Little Porcupine. "Grab your toes, Papa, 'cause here goes!"

## Big Porcupine's Picnic

Now, Papa, one day the Big Porcupine in the Sky said, "It is sleepy time. It is story time. All the little porcupines on the earth need to hear a story before they go to sleep.

"But how can I tell them a story? I am up here and they are down there. I don't make big boom-boom noises like the thunderclouds. Even if I did, the little porcupines would never hear me. Oh me, oh my. I must think of something."

The Big Porcupine in the Sky thought and thought.

"I know," he said, "since I can't tell them a story, I will give them a picnic."

So the Big Porcupine in the Sky got a big basket from his big cloud cupboard. Then he pulled out a big green blanket from his cloud chest and put it into the basket—just so.

Then he went out into his sky garden and picked some grapes and bananas, putting the grapes on top of the bananas—just so.

Then he went into his berry patch and filled his handkerchief with red raspberries. Then he tied the handkerchief at the top—just like you do, Papa. Then he set down the raspberry bundle on the grapes—just so.

"Now," he said, "I will take my picnic basket to my favorite place."
Big Porcupine hurried over to a patch of blue sky way out West.
There, he emptied his basket and spread his green blanket along the
edge of the sky.

"Now," he said, "I will kneel down and begin my picnic."

First, he took the bundle of raspberries and squashed it down over his head. Squisssssssssssh. So all the juice dribbled down his face. Dribble, dribble, dribble, until his whole face was red.

Then he wrapped the grapes in the handkerchief and squeezed it. Ooooooooooooze went the purple juice. Then he wiped the purple grape juice across the whole sky.

Za-weep!

Then he peeled a banana, and made a yellow line of peels right under the green blanket—just so.

"There," he said. "That is my picnic, and I hope all the little creatures like it."

Well, Papa, when the little creatures looked up, they saw the first sunset ever in the world. And it was so beautiful, they cheered.

And from that day on, that is how the Big Porcupine in the Sky told his stories. With sunsets. The sunsets are Big Porcupine's picnics in the sky.

"Wow," says Papa Porcupine. "That was a good story. And I guess that is one picnic where nobody is ever left out."

"Yes," says Little Porcupine, "and when I have a picnic, I'll invite everyone too. Even Fox."

"Well," says Papa Porcupine, "that would be a kindly thing to do."

"Yes," says Little Porcupine, "and then do you think Fox would be my friend?"

"He might," says Papa Porcupine. "He might get to know what a bright toesy little porcupine you are. Now don't you think it's time you went to sleep?"

"Just one more story," says Little Porcupine. He gives Papa Porcupine a big scratchy hug.

"Which one?" says Papa Porcupine.

"The one about Big Porcupine and the Moon. If you tell that one, I'll close my eyes real tight and pretend to sleep."

"A super idea," says Papa Porcupine. "Keep them closed and grab your toes."

# How the Big Porcupine Fooled the Moon

Moon was jealous of the Big Porcupine in the Sky.
"He's brighter than I am," he moaned to Owl. "Big Porcupine's
bigger, he's warmer, and he gets to shine all day."

"Well, he is the Sun," said Owl. "That's the way things are."

"It isn't fair," said Moon. "I can't help it if I'm small. I can't help it if I shine only at night. Big Porcupine makes me so mad I eat too many cloud muffins. I have to go on a diet to count off the weeks."

"That's not his fault," said Owl.

"Yes it is," said Moon. "And I will get him."

"Be careful you don't get yourself," said Owl, and off she flew.

So one night, Moon pulled his night cloak down over the Big Porcupine in the Sky while he slept.

"Whoopee," Moon said, "no one will ever see him again."

Moon never thought about Big Porcupine's rays. Those rays shot out like spears and poked the Moon's cloak full of holes.

Moon was so angry he ate four cloud muffins without thinking. Before he knew it, he was one full moon.

"You are mean Porcupine," Moon cried. "You have poked my beautiful cloak full of holes."

"I'm sorry, Moon," said Big Porcupine, "but those holes will help me guard against your night tricks."

To this day, holes are still up there. They are the stars.
At night, it is Big Porcupine who is shining through
the dark cloak of the sky. That is how he watches over all the
Little Porcupines in the world.

"Even me, Papa?" says Little Porcupine, opening one eye.

"Yes, especially you."

Little Porcupine gives Papa Porcupine a big prickly hug.

"Then maybe I will go to sleep," he says.